The Ultimate Christmas Creativity Book

Illustrated by: CCA and B, LLC Storybook Artists

Inspired by the art and character designs of *The Elf on the Shelf*®

Based on *The Elf on the Shelf*® by Carol Aebersold and Chanda A. Bell.

Printed in China.

SNOWMAN

```
A C M Y F J H T E L H E O X K
M I T T E N S K B I N S U V K
I M O F E K A R U J Q Q C T K
S L P Q D L Z V T Y O Y I E R
I F S T F L G V T D E O N H G
X H X W T P O E O D J X N C U
Y N O Z Q E S Z N L V E K C F
D N N V C F P N S G W L D W P
S D Y G E C R G O A T U F X X
X M V Q A U X A O W T P L I F
Y R H R U B C G C A M B B T U
V Y R T G J O U H S E A H Q F
N O K W A W A P X G C E N Q Y
T M A G I C L R V T N M A T Z
X M I Y L Z R E A R N H E C W
```

BUTTONS   **CARROT**   **COAL**

HAT   **MAGIC**   **MITTENS**

SCARF   **SNOWFLAKE**   **SNOWMAN**

Draw your room
below the flying elf.

Draw a path through the North Pole.

NORTH POLE

Decorate the plate of cookies.

E is for elf

Draw all of your favorite foods and snacks in the pantry.

FLOUR

SUGAR

Fill the bowl with candy.

Draw yourself riding a bike with the elf, but don't forget your helmet!

How do you think the elf feels?
Write your answer in the blank. Then color the elf.

1. _____

2. _____

3. _____

4. _____

10

Decorate the
gingerbread man.

12

What fun things are in
this wallet?

AMOUNT:

$

GIFT CARD

NORTH POLE CANDY CARD
1000 1000 1000 100

NORTH POLE IDENTIFICATION

ELFIE C. ELFMAN
CANDY CANE LANE
NORTH POLE

BIRTHDAY: 12/24/03   HEIGHT: 12"
HAIR COLOR: BROWN   EYES : BLUE

SIGNATURE: elfie

ID#: 123456789

What is this elf imagining?

Decorate the sign.

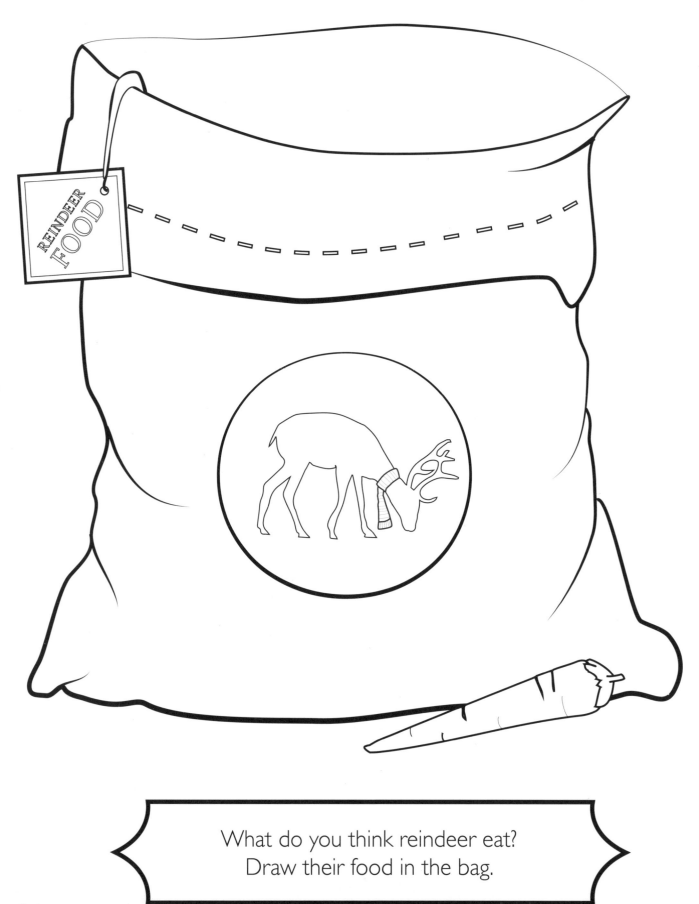

REINDEER FOOD

What do you think reindeer eat?
Draw their food in the bag.

How many elves are in Santa's study? _____

Draw Christmas scenes
in the snow globes.

Decorate the tree with the following:

- 1 string of garland
- 3 gingerbread men
- 6 ornaments
- 1 star
- 3 candy canes
- 1 elf

Can you unscramble these words?
Hint: They are all drinks elves love!
Then draw your favorite drink on the cart.

1. _____
   toh hoaceltoc

2. _____
   kiml

3. _____
   kmilshaek

4. _____
   occao

5. _____
   negogg

6. _____
   alpep redci

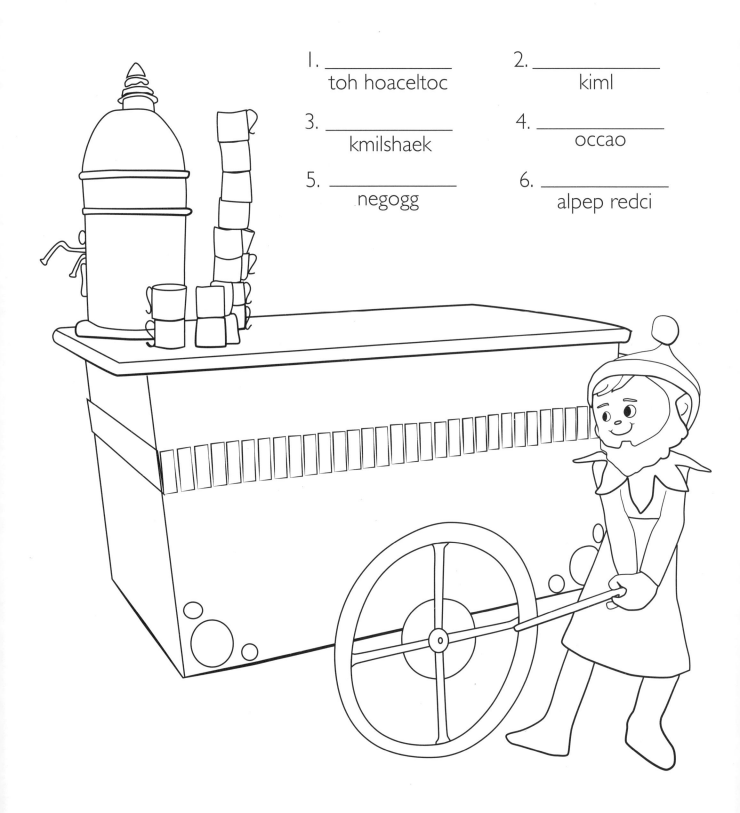

20

Which stocking belongs to this elf?
Follow the clues to find out!

- It does not have hearts or a bow
- It does not have stars or stripes
- It is not small
- It does not have a curly toe
- It does not have a Christmas tree

What is this elf
eating for dinner?

22

Draw hot chocolate in this mug.
Don't forget the marshmallows!

Color these balloons with fun patterns and colors.

Draw another act of
kindness above.

Decorate this elf cookie to match the one on the right!

These elves are roasting marshmallows at night. Draw some stars and the moon.

Can you find the following items?

2 elves	2 snowflakes
2 stars	7 bows
1 mitten	4 candy canes

This elf can't remember where
he left the gifts!
Help him find them!

Color this
snowman.
Give him an
expression.

Connect the dots to see the elf.

On each string there is a decoration
that doesn't match the others.
Can you find all three?

CHRISTMAS DECORATIONS

```
E F T C R X B G H E O J H I S
A O S T N E M A N R O I O E G
I S T L V R O H W F H K L C X
D N E E S I F G G B R D L I R
A R T K L P X O G Y N K Y J W
X E C I X T W L S A J W V D Q
D T B U N Y S T C S E A S F G
E N D I A S O I R I B B O N S
S A I S K C E L M B A E I T E
G L M K K E R L H D R F X W D
F Y Z I G M K U B K S Z P O U
K P N H U C P E E V J G I I H
K G F Q L U L V U K W V J X X
S K Y U N L S N S G J G Q K N
O Y E K S H N F K K G A W M W
```

BELLS   CANDLES   HOLLY
LANTERNS   MISTLETOE   ORNAMENTS
RIBBONS   STOCKINGS   TINSEL

33

Help the elf take the right path to the finish line!

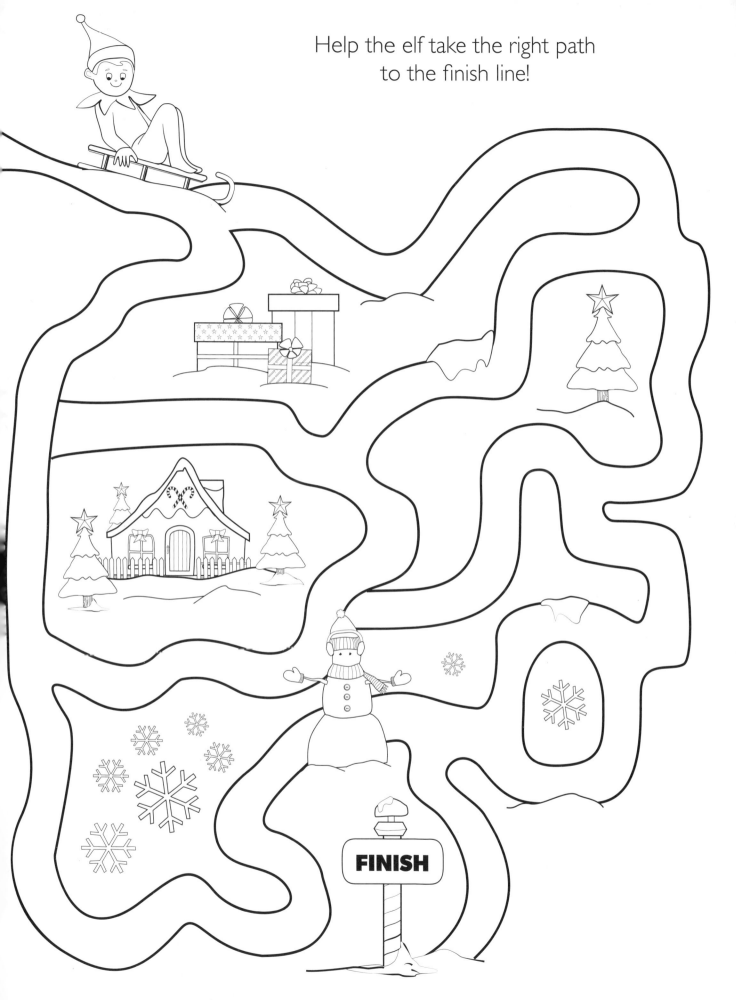

FINISH

START

How many more lights go on this tree? Follow the path and add the numbers to find out!

3

2

1

7

4

6

5

=

What doesn't belong in this bag with the other gifts? Color the whole scene.

Which one of these names belongs to this elf?
Follow the clues below to find out!

- It does not start with an "E"
- It has two syllables
- It is not a Christmas name
- It does not have five letters
- It does not start with "T"

Jingle

Max

Elfie

Louis

Tucker

Peanut

Edward

HELLO
my name is:

38

Complete this maze to help the elf place the star on top of the tree!

Only one mitten is finished.
Follow the yarn to find out which one.

1.   2.   3.   4.   5.

40

Fill in the following tiles to see the Christmas picture below!
Cross off the numbers as you draw them in.

(Ex) K: 2-22   Q: 14-17   L: 19-22   I: 5-17   J: 3-17

D: 17   L: 3-17   N: 7-17   M: 5-17   J: 19-22

E: 14-17   H: 7-17   P: 11-17   I: 19-22   O: 9-17

R: 17   F: 11-17   G: 9-17   M: 19-22

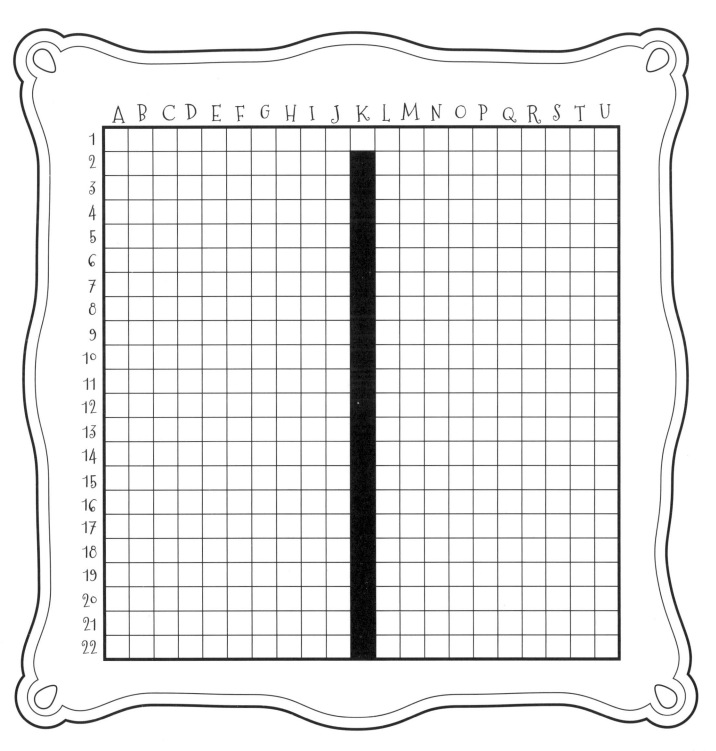

The weather at the North Pole is cold with lots of snow! You decide what the weather will be like for two days.

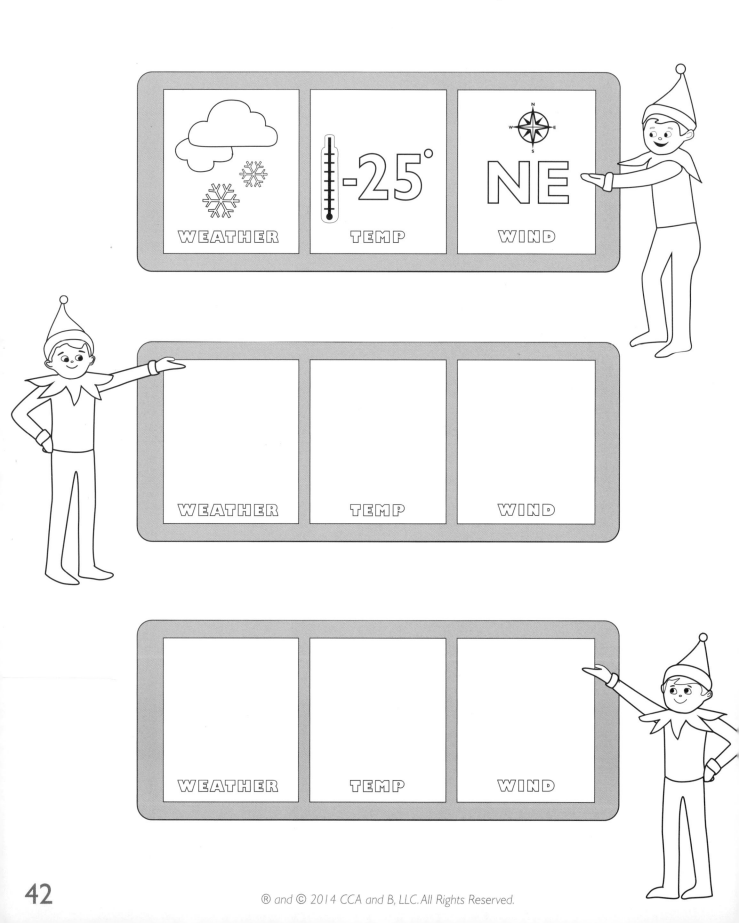

Which one of these snowflakes does not have a match?

What do you think the boy is saying to the elf? Draw a picture on the bulletin board.

Draw your favorite
snowflake shape.

What is the elf thinking?

Color the crayons with your favorite colors.

The elf sees himself in the mirror.
Can you draw his reflection?

48

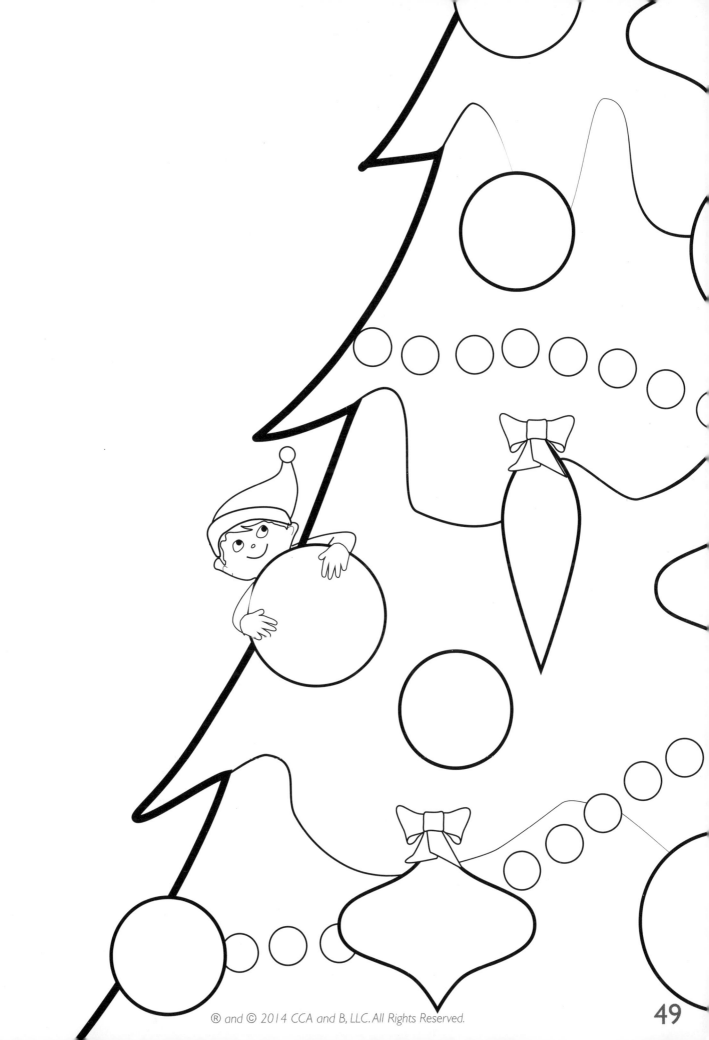

This elf is having so much fun sledding!
Draw more trees and snow around him.

WINTER ACTIVITIES

```
Y N K E C I S U B V S S S R
N F T J D K O A R L E L N W C
V T J L I O N K E G I E O I M
P Y F I E V M I E W F G W C T
I G N U Z B G Q O X S N B E W
B G N K K H A N N Y F A O F W
E C O I R P Q T R D R W A I E
S G N I T A K S E C I O R S E
Q L D J P A P P E H M N D H H
D E E Q Z O R L S E Z S I I C
S W H D C A R O L I N G N N F
D U N M D R S T C K M R G G W
F W M X X I N M C E Y Y X E A
V C F E W N N H C X D M U S W
K U Z R G N B G U I N N D D P
```

CAROLING   DECORATING   SNOWBOARDING
ICE SKATING   SKIING   SLEDDING
SLEIGH RIDES   SNOW ANGELS   ICE FISHING

Can you find all these winter activity words?

51

Finish the shadow on the elf.
The elf flying is already done for you.

Decorate the bulletin board.

Draw fish in the pond for the elf to catch.

54

Finish the other side of
the elf's face.

What's inside all the jars?

Write your name on the left stocking,
then decorate both stockings.

What acts of kindness go on the nice list?

NICE LIST

_____

_____

_____

_____

_____

_____

_____

OFFICIAL SEAL

NORTH POLE

Follow the instructions below
to learn how to draw your
own snowflake.

1. Find your favorite pen or marker and
draw a straight line.

2. Draw two lines to intersect the line
you just drew. They don't have to be
perfect. Every snowflake is unique!

3. Now, at every end, draw two short lines.

4. Practice drawing them in the empty space!

60

Decorate and write on these gift tags.

It's time for the elf to take a trip! Help him pack by drawing all the things in his suitcase. One is done for you.

1. toothbrush
2. pajamas
3. candy canes
4. ~~teddy bear~~
5. ice skates
6. elf hat

ELF

Draw the faces on the elves.

EXCITED

SURPRISED

HAPPY

One of these presents has something different about it.
Can you find which one is different?

Decorate the wreath.

How tall is this elf? _____
How tall are you? _____

9 8 7 6 5 4 3 2 1

This elf needs candy to fill up his stocking. Complete the maze to get to the candy in the center!

Color the elf's doodles in his sketchpad.

Now draw your own doodles.

The elves are having a
snowball fight!
Draw more snowballs.

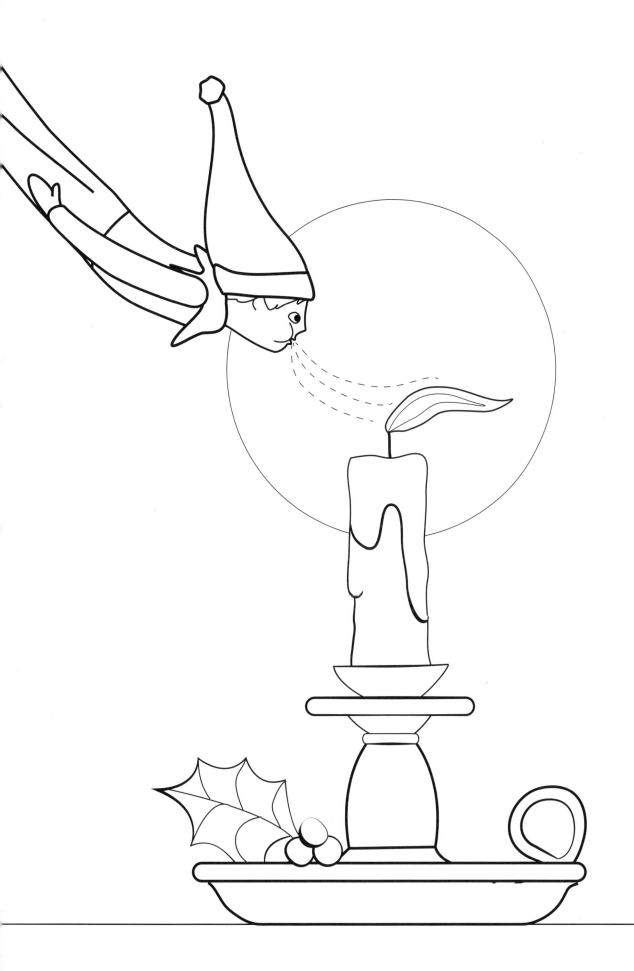

72

Color this fun kitchen scene!

1 CUP

73

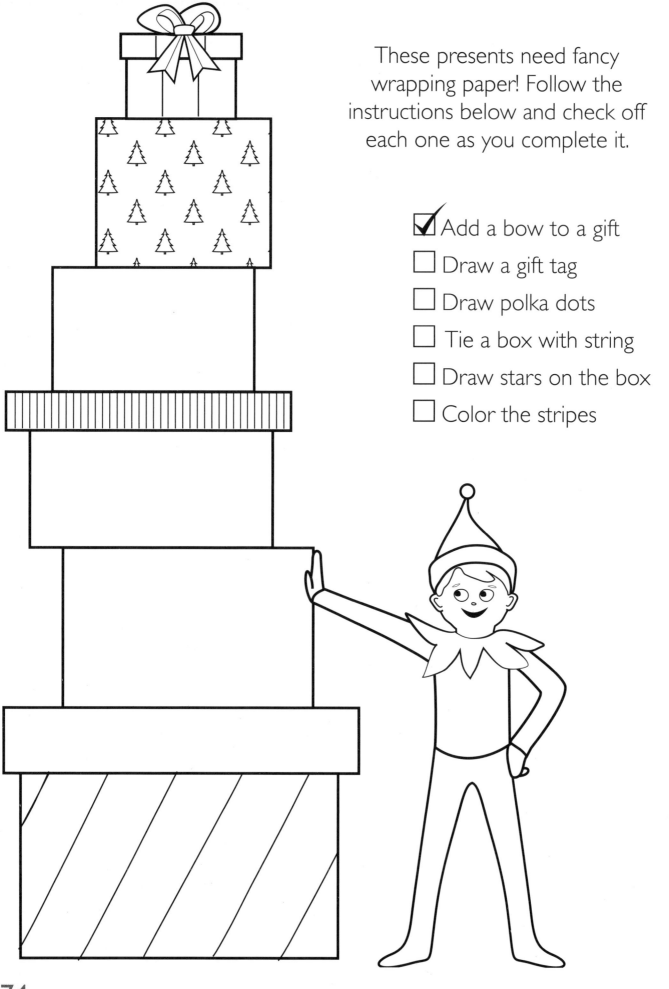

These presents need fancy wrapping paper! Follow the instructions below and check off each one as you complete it.

☑ Add a bow to a gift

☐ Draw a gift tag

☐ Draw polka dots

☐ Tie a box with string

☐ Draw stars on the box

☐ Color the stripes

74

What is on
Santa's sleigh?

Color this December calendar.

DECEMBER

SU	M	T	W	TH	F	S
1	2	3	4	5	6	7
8	9	10	11	12	13	14
15	16	17	18	19	20	21
22	23	24	25			

The elf hears something on the roof!
Draw what you think it might be.

Can you find all the things listed in this holiday scene?

- 4 pieces of holly
- 4 candy canes
- 4 snowflakes
- 4 stars

Which elf is holding which balloon?
Trace the strings to find out!

1.

2.

3.

4.

5.

Jingle

Elfie

Fred

Enrique

Howie

What are these elves
talking about?

The elf tripped and
spilled all of the ornaments!
How many are there?
Draw over the outlines and
color as you count them.

What clothes are in the elf's closet?

The elf can't decide which skirt to wear!
Color and design these three skirts,
and then pick your favorite.

Draw animals you would find at the North Pole!

What is sitting on the shelf
next to this elf?

85

There are four differences between these two scenes.
Can you spot them all?

Decorate your own stockings!

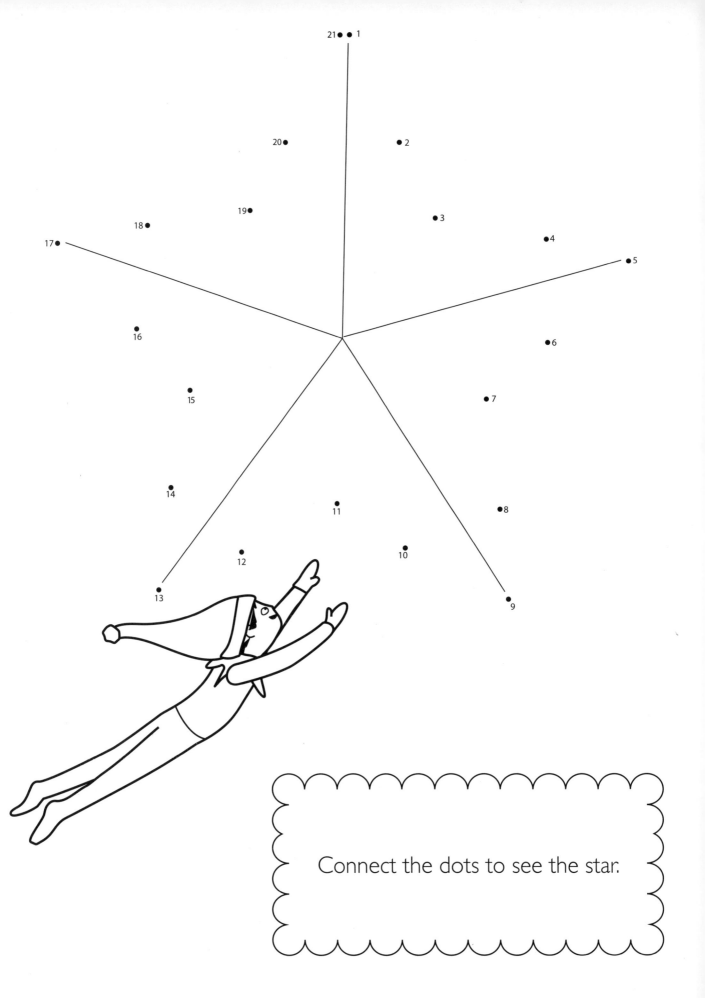

Connect the dots to see the star.

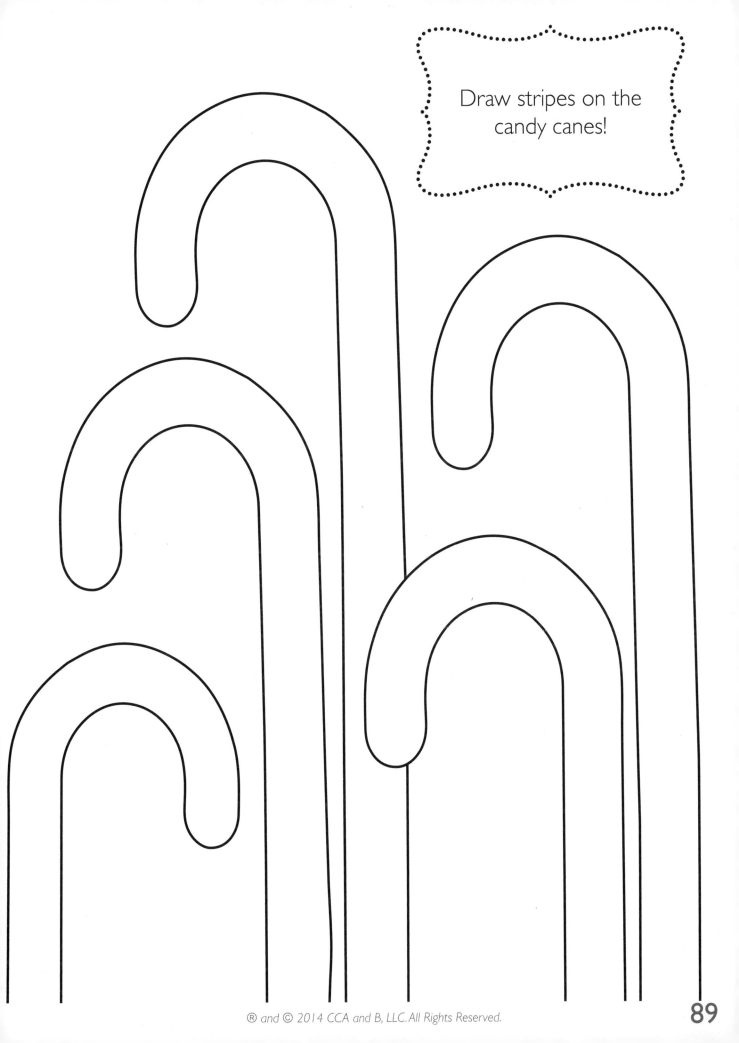

Draw stripes on the candy canes!

ORANGE

YELLOW

RED

GREEN

BLUE

Color these ornaments!

90

Help the elves by wrapping
this present.

There are elves hiding in the bookshelf!
Can you find them all?

Draw this elf's dream!

Each of the objects below is shaded.
What fraction of the Christmas object is shaded?
Write your answer in the blank provided!

$= \dfrac{1}{4}$

Draw pictures of you and your friends in the frames.

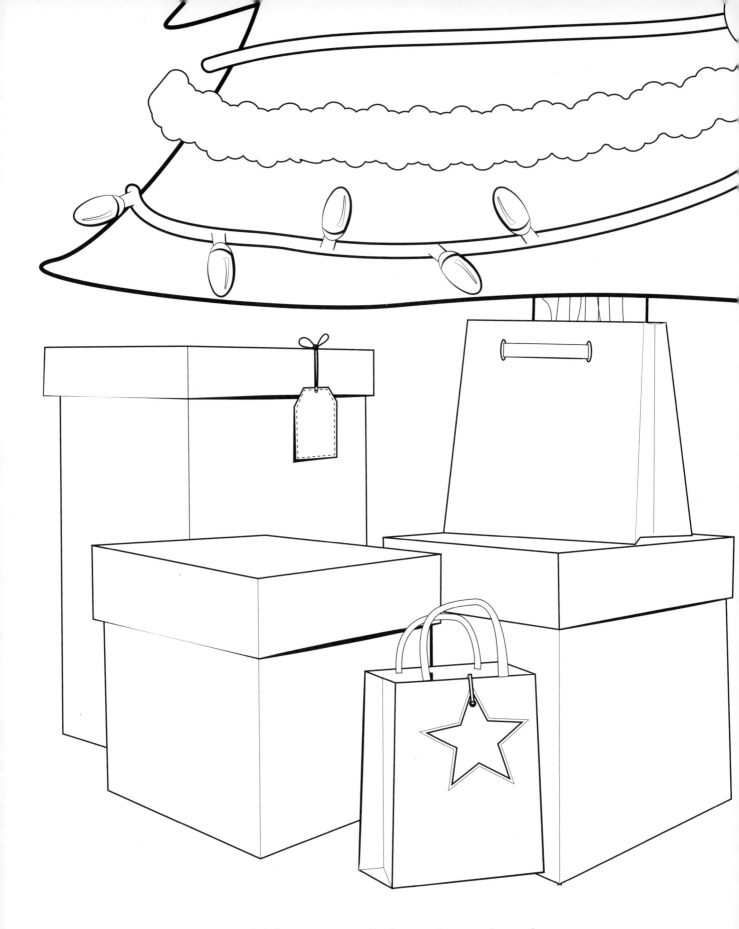

Where are all these bags from?
Write and design the labels and patterns.

Which one of these hats belongs to the elf?
Use the clues to find out!

- It does not have a bow
- It is not the smallest
- It is not the biggest

- It does not have stripes
- It does not have a pattern
- It does not have a patch

LETTER TO SANTA:

Complete the crossword by writing in the word
that matches the picture in the number spot.

ACROSS

3
6
8
9
10
11

DOWN

1
2
4
5
7

Can you help the elf spot which cookie on each plate is different from the others?

CHRISTMAS TREATS

```
Q C V E M W C X Y P D C T S E
K T A U F H E P U A U H J N T
A L N N O J G B E N D E M A A
B S I W D L Z R M T D S B X L
R G Y F D Y B D F D B T Q Z O
C A N H J R C R A D N N G Y C
V G W I E A U A J N Z U R L O
V A E G D I K U N R Q T X R H
D A N O T D P W P E S S S F C
X I E C M M U M N J G G K N T
G U A W D Y Y P K S U A L V O
Y K F D J X Y Q Z R K S Z B H
E L E X Q S G B E N L W L V I
S E I K O O C K F O I I B N E
P E P P E R M I N T M D V T V
```

Can you find all the Christmas treat words?

CANDY CANE   CHESTNUTS   COOKIES

FRUITCAKE   MILK   PUDDING

GINGERBREAD   PEPPERMINT   HOT CHOCOLATE

These elves love their winter scarves!
Color their scarves with fun and bright patterns.

All of these stockings need candy, but how much?
Solve the problems to see how much each stocking gets,
then draw in the candy!

$12 - 3 =$ **9**
STOCKING 1

$8 - 4 =$ [ ]
STOCKING 2

$3 + 7 =$ [ ]
STOCKING 3

$9 + 3 =$ [ ]
STOCKING 4

$15 - 6 =$ [ ]
STOCKING 5

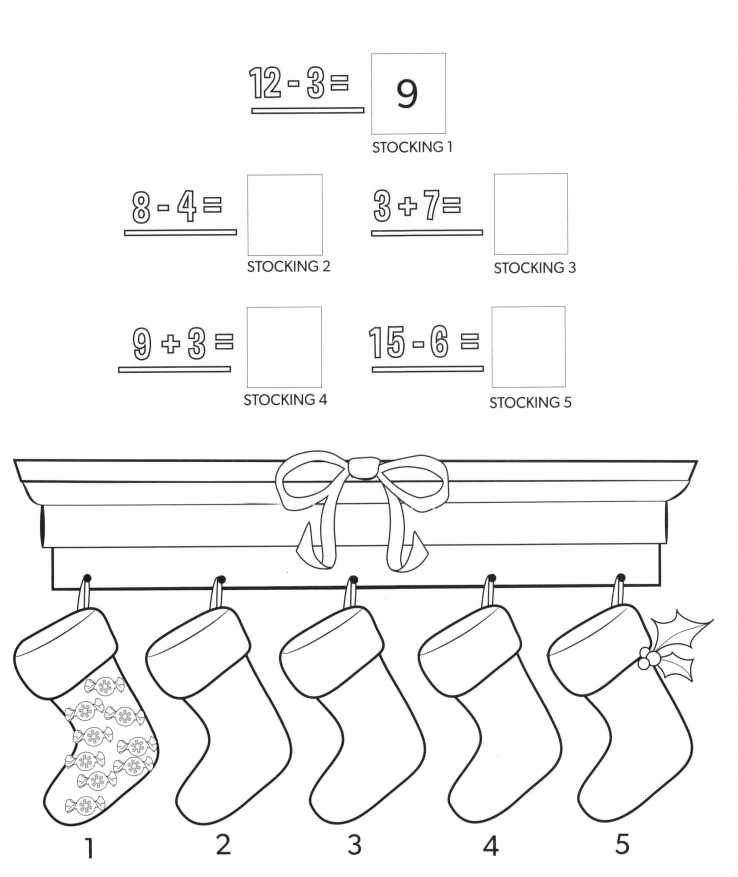

1   2   3   4   5

Draw a silly hat on this elf.

104

Help the elf get more snow to the snowman before he melts! Collect as many snowflakes as you can along the way.

A=1
B=2
C=3
D=4
E=5
F=6
G=7
H=8
I=9
J=10
K=11
L=12
M=13
N=14
O=15
P=16
Q=17
R=18
S=19
T=20
U=21
V=22
W=23
X=24
Y=25
Z=26

Using the decoding key to the left, decode Santa's message to the elf!

__ __ __ __ __ __   __ __ __ __ __ __ __ __ __
19 16 18 5 1 4   3 8 18 9 19 20 13 1 19

__ __ __   __ __   __ __ __   __ __ __
10 15 25   20 15   1 12 12   20 8 5

__ __ __ __ __   __ __ __   __ __ __ __
 7 9 18 12 19   1 14 4   2 15 25 19

106

Follow the path of lights
to get to the tree.

Fill in the following tiles to see the Christmas picture below!
Cross off the numbers as you draw them in.

(Ex)F:2	B:6	D:12	M:9	J:6	G:3	G:7	H:9	J:8	H:4	H:13
J:14	N:10	L:4	J:2	F:6	I:13	I:9	C:8	K:8	H:5
C:3	B:10	C:9	F:14	J:10	I:3	I:7	M:8	L:8	H:6
M:13	N:6	M:7	E:5	K:5	G:13	G:9	D:8	G:8	H:10
D:4	C:13	E:11	K:11	H:14	B:8	H:8	E:8	I:8	H:11
L:12	M:3	C:7	F:10	H:2	N:8	H:7	F:8	H3	H:12

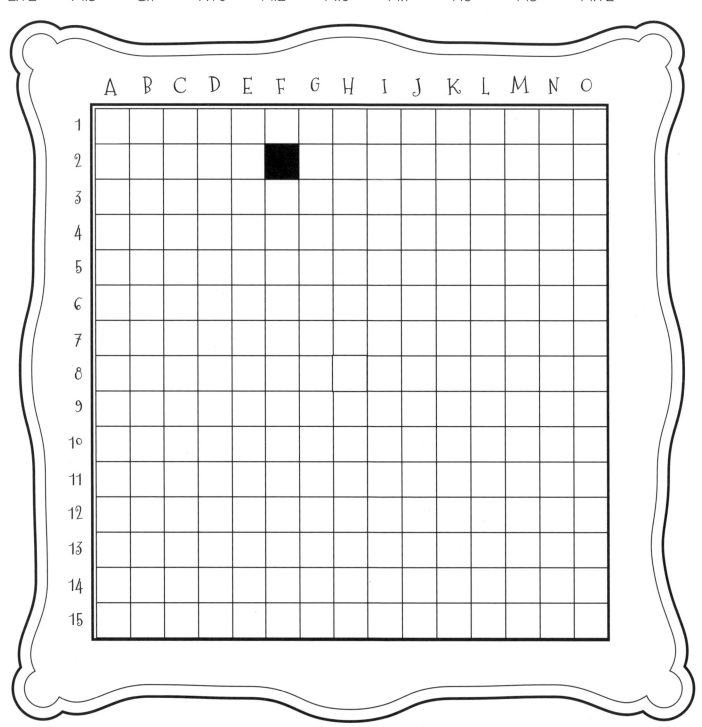

Each of these elves has two gifts.
Guess each of their gifts by the clues they give.

My gifts make music
_____
_____

My gifts are used to
draw pictures
_____
_____

My gifts have wheels
_____
_____

My gifts are used to
play sports
_____
_____

Christmas List

Can you find all the Christmas tree words?

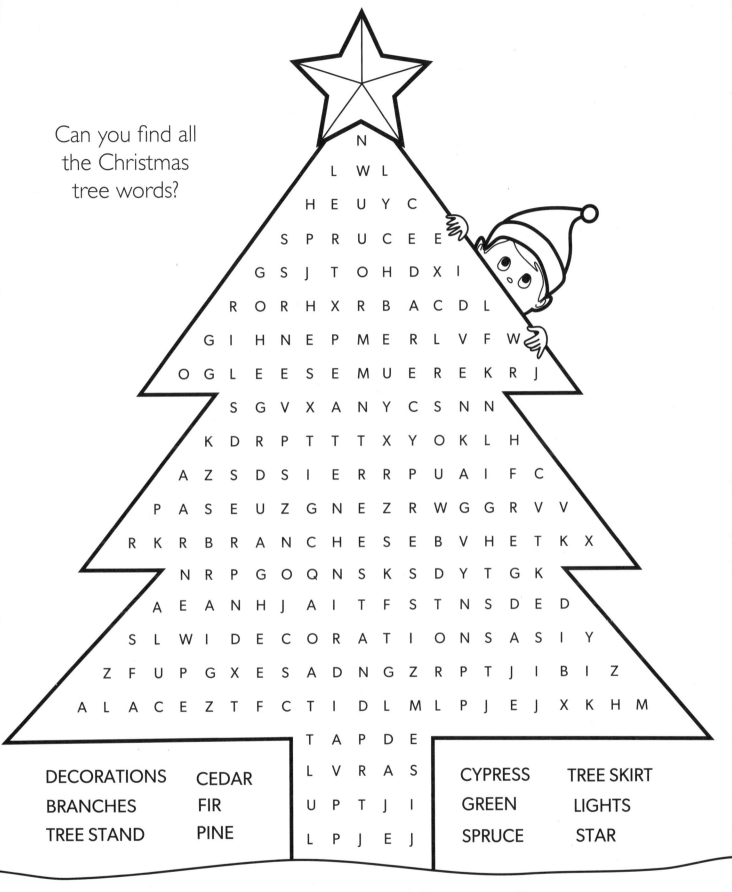

N
L W L
H E U Y C
S P R U C E E
G S J T O H D X I
R O R H X R B A C D L
G I H N E P M E R L V F W
O G L E E S E M U E R E K R J
S G V X A N Y C S N N
K D R P T T T X Y O K L H
A Z S D S I E R R P U A I F C
P A S E U Z G N E Z R W G G R V V
R K R B R A N C H E S E B V H E T K X
N R P G O Q N S K S D Y T G K
A E A N H J A I T F S T N S D E D
S L W I D E C O R A T I O N S A S I Y
Z F U P G X E S A D N G Z R P T J I B I Z
A L A C E Z T F C T I D L M L P J E J X K H M
T A P D E
L V R A S
U P T J I
L P J E J

DECORATIONS	CEDAR	
BRANCHES	FIR	
TREE STAND	PINE	

CYPRESS	TREE SKIRT
GREEN	LIGHTS
SPRUCE	STAR

CHRISTMAS TREE

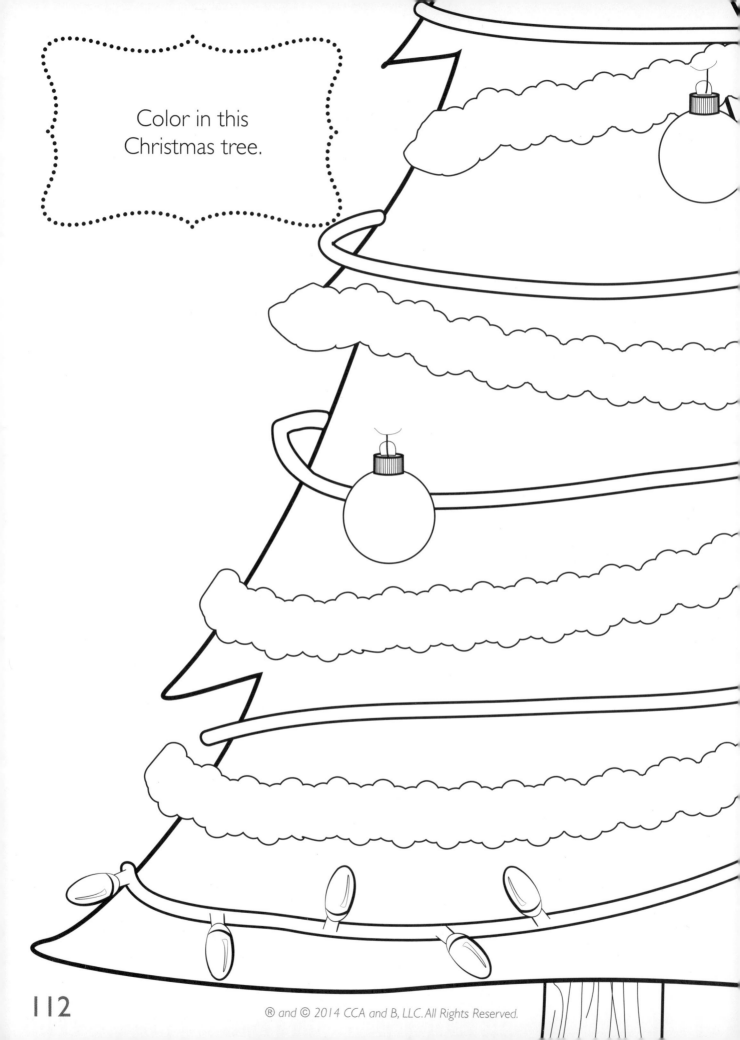

Color in this Christmas tree.

Which mitten doesn't
have a matching pattern?

Help this scout elf get to the
North Pole by finishing his path.
What's in his letter?

FROM:

SANTA

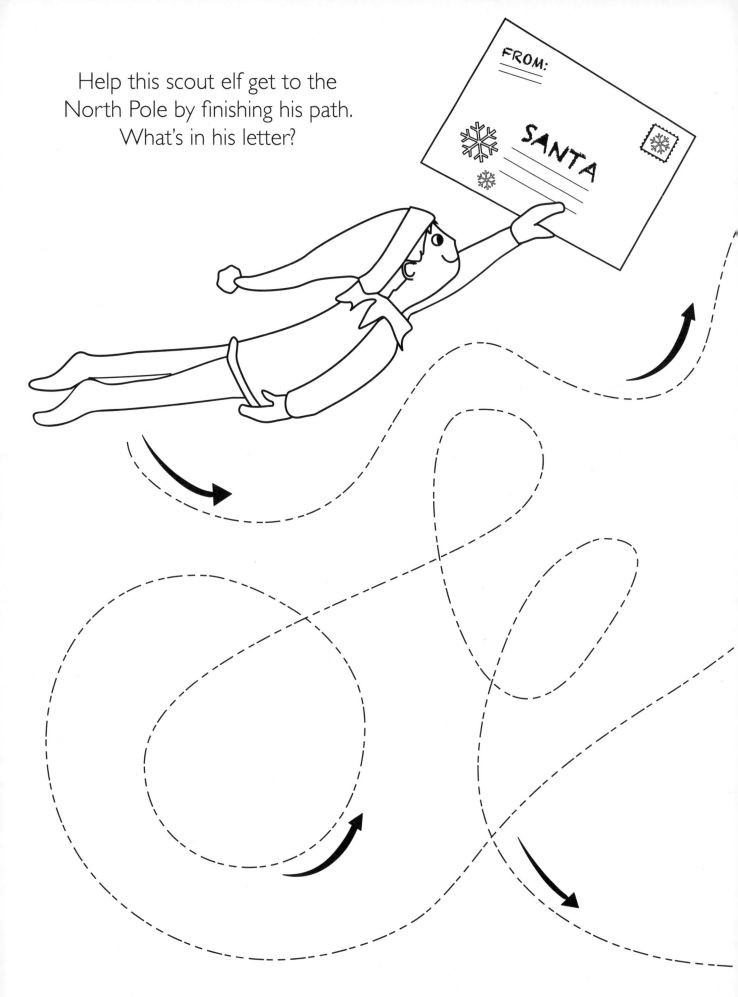

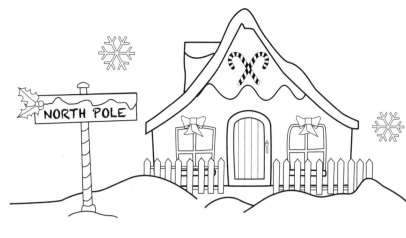

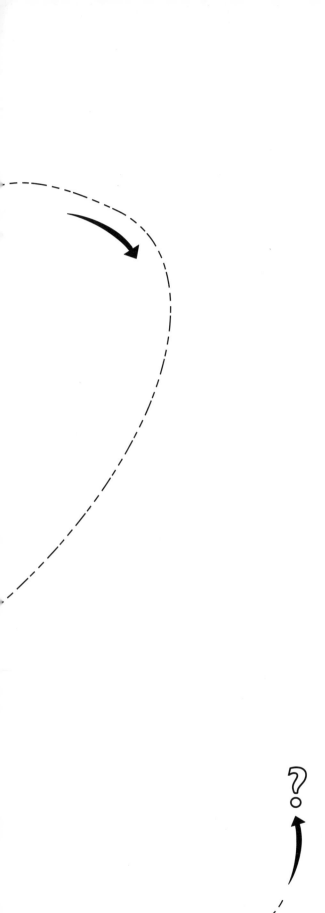

Unscramble each of the clue words. Take the letters that appear in the circles and unscramble them for the final word!

ESGHIL

NTESRPE

LYOHL

ATREHW

ANSWER:

____ ____ ____ ____ ____

Answer Key

Page 2

BUTTONS
HAT
SCARF

CARROT
MAGIC
SNOWFLAKE

COAL
MITTENS
SNOWMAN

Page 10

1. Surprised
2. Sad
3. Tired
4. Happy

Page 11

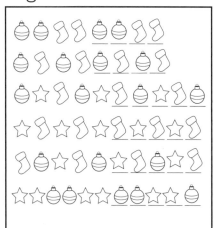

Page 17

There are 5 elves in Santa's study.

Page 20

1. Hot chocolate
2. Milk
3. Milkshake
4. Cocoa
5. Eggnog
6. Apple Cider

Page 21

This stocking belongs to the elf.

Page 28

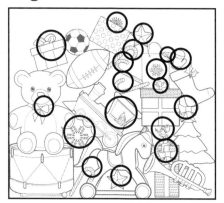

Page 29

Page 32

Page 33

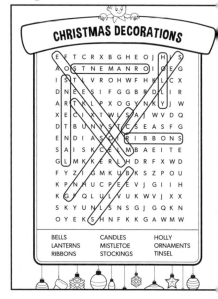

BELLS
LANTERNS
RIBBONS

CANDLES
MISTLETOE
STOCKINGS

HOLLY
ORNAMENTS
TINSEL

Page 35

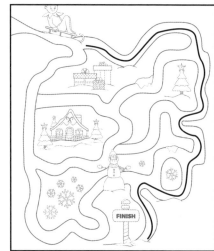

118

Answer Key

Page 36

28 more lights go on the Christmas tree.

Page 37

The fish does not belong.

Page 38

The elf's name is Peanut.

Page 39

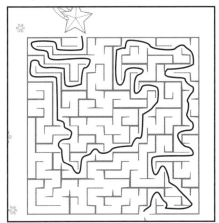

Page 40

Mitten 5 is not yet done.

Page 41

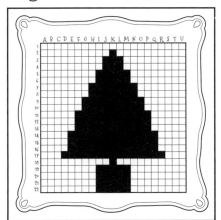

Page 43

This snowflake does not have a match.

Page 51

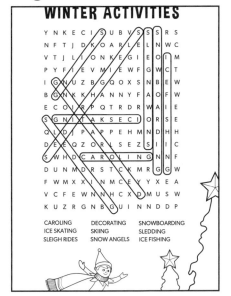

WINTER ACTIVITIES

CAROLING
ICE SKATING
SLEIGH RIDES
DECORATING
SKIING
SNOW ANGELS
SNOWBOARDING
SLEDDING
ICE FISHING

Page 64

The present in the center is different; its ribbon is folded four times.

Page 66

The elf is 7 inches tall.

Page 67

Page 78

Page 79

Jingle has balloon #2.
Elfie has balloon #4.
Fred has balloon #5.
Enrique has balloon #3.
Howie has balloon #1.

Page 81

There are 10 ornaments that the elf spilled.

Page 86

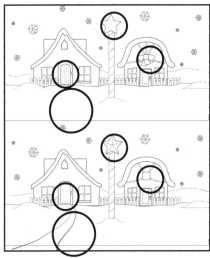

Answer Key

Page 92

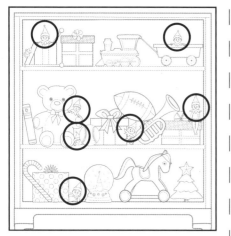

Page 94

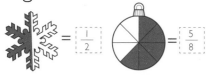

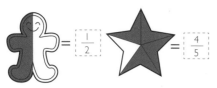

Page 97

This hat is the elf's.

Page 99

Down
1. Snowflake
2. Gift
4. Ornament
5. Santa
7. Stocking

Across
3. Cookies
6. Bow
8. Star
9. Candy Cane
10. Candle
11. Tree

Page 100

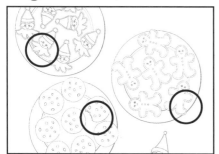

Page 101

CHRISTMAS TREATS

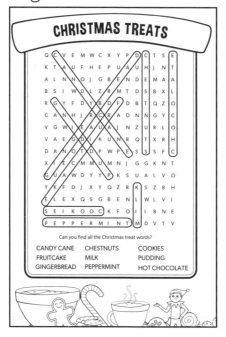

Can you find all the Christmas treat words?

CANDY CANE	CHESTNUTS	COOKIES
FRUITCAKE	MILK	PUDDING
GINGERBREAD	PEPPERMINT	HOT CHOCOLATE

Page 103

8 − 4 = 4

9 + 3 = 12

3 + 7 = 10

15 − 6 = 9

Page 105

Page 106

The message says "Spread Christmas joy to all the girls and boys."

Page 108

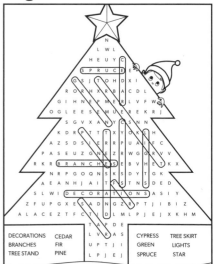

Page 109

Music: trumpet, drum
Drawing: crayons, pencil
Wheels: train, wagon
Sports: football, baseball

Page 111

DECORATIONS	CEDAR	CYPRESS	TREE SKIRT
BRANCHES	FIR	GREEN	LIGHTS
TREE STAND	PINE	SPRUCE	STAR

Page 113

This mitten does not have a match.

Page 116

ESGHIL = Sleigh
NTESRPE = Present
LYOHL = Holly
ATREHW = Wreath
Answer: Snow

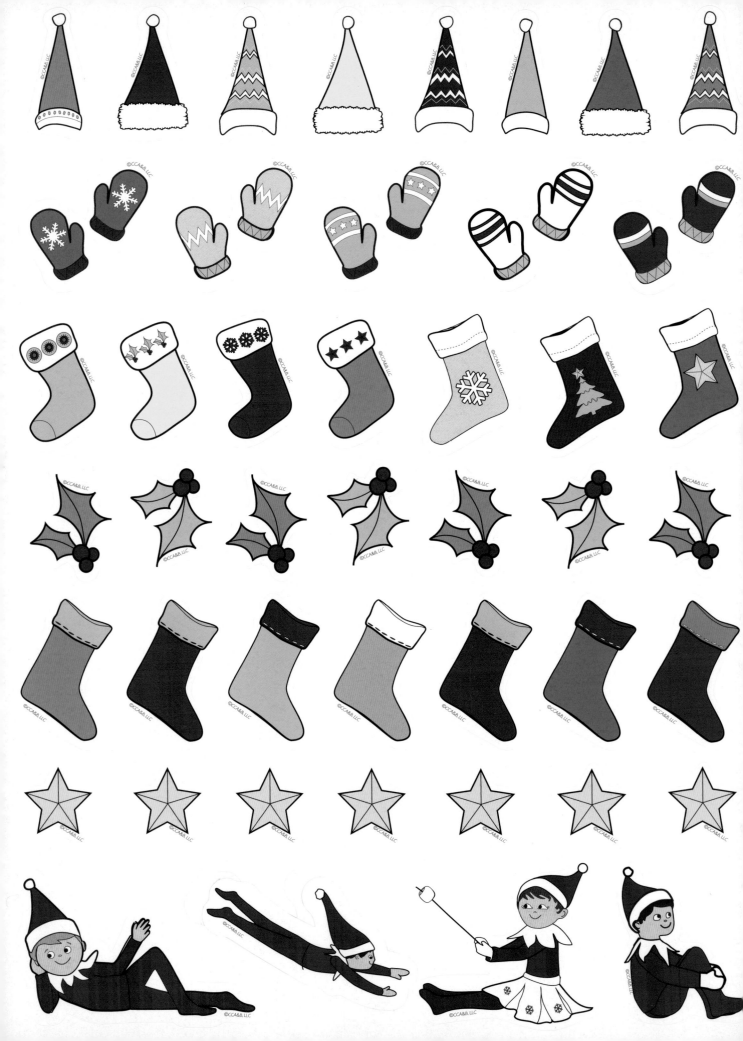

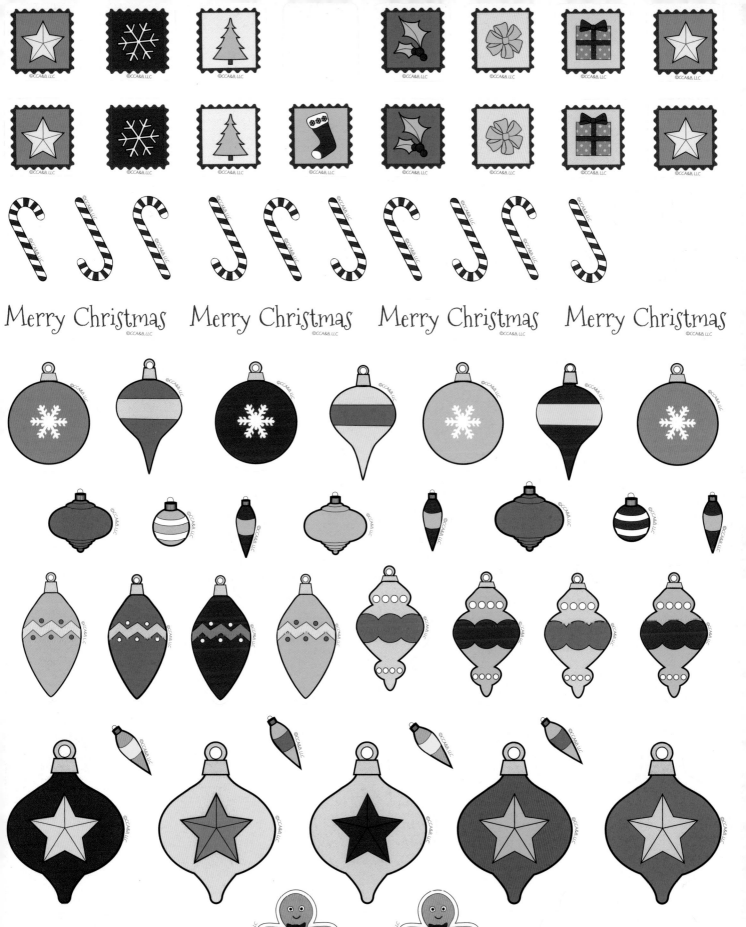

Merry Christmas Merry Christmas Merry Christmas Merry Christmas